The Grate Adventure of Lester Lester Zester

Mark Dantzler

Illustrated by
Julia Pelikhovich

The Grate Adventure of Lester Zester
Copyright © 2021 by Mark Dantzler
ISBN 9781645383000
First Edition

The Grate Adventure of Lester Zester
by Mark Dantzler
Illustrated by Julia Pelikhovich
Cover Design/Typography by Kaeley Dunteman

For information, please contact:

www.orangehatpublishing.com
Waukesha, WI

For Cindy

Of chocolate tortes and rugelach treats;
Hot icing on scones–such decadent sweets!
For butterhorn crescents rolled out with care;
Her kitchen is proof a baker lives there.

The magic of the winter holidays brought Lester to his forever-family home. The young zester was wrapped in a festive foil pattern of candy stripes and buried beneath a splendid fir, with instructions to remain silent until Christmas morning.

Lester was eager
to prove his
trustworthiness, but he
found himself humming
aloud to the joyful
carols that were sung
throughout the house.
Hoping to join the curious
array of helpful tools at
work in Chef's kitchen,
Lester worried that
he might be forgotten
among the trove of
impressive gifts.

Lester was a brand-new zester: a microplane zester-grater, to be precise. He didn't care for the title microplane, though. As far as he knew, he couldn't fly and had no plans to try. Proudly assembled in the USA, Lester came with a stainless-steel blade covered with tiny cutting holes. His bottom half was attached to a black plastic handle.

Lester had assumed that he was inexpensive because the home-goods store where he was displayed had advertised him as a *must-have stocking-stuffer*. His packaging described him as being versatile and built-to-last, which he hoped to be true. As a novice tool in a real kitchen, Lester wasn't entirely sure what a zester's job required.

Christmas came, and
Lester was unwrapped
at last, giving him a first
glimpse of his new home.
He quickly learned that
each useful tool had a
unique *kitchen purpose*.
It was rumored that all
new arrivals would be
assigned to live in one of
two places: the *Everyday
Drawer*, a happy place
for novel and helpful
items, or the *Gadget Box*,
a mysterious container
used for discarding
unwanted kitchen tools.

Hidden inside the old pantry, this foreboding place was where last-minute gifts, gadgets, and gizmos disappeared forever! Lester longed to be useful and to understand his true kitchen purpose.

Chef's kitchen was sun-lit and airy. At one end, there was a shiny double wall oven with clever knobs and dials and a digital timer. In the center of the room stood a custom cook island with all manner of spices carefully arranged on top. Some of them had traveled from exotic places and wore impressive labels, like tarragon, marjoram, and basil.

Resting at the far end of the kitchen was a large wooden breakfast table. At some point, its four tired legs had dutifully served as scratching posts for the house cat. The floor was clean, with a pattern of white porcelain square tiles that were handmade in a far-off land called Italy.

Each morning, Chef's kitchen awakened to a kaleidoscope of inviting sights, smells, and sounds. Grandparents gathered to gossip while sipping something spicy; pots and pans constantly clanged as amateur cooks collided; there was scooping and spilling and sifting and stirring from tin containers brimming with sugar and sea salt; cumulus clouds of flour softly settled upon unsuspecting countertops; small sneakers squeaked as children chased children; a welcome aroma of buttery, baked bread was served with jars of jam and jelly; and music and conversation brought eruptions of laughter from all corners. This kitchen was so full of love and life— it is where Lester was meant to be!

Chef was the lady of the house. A tall, lovely woman with wispy, wavy hair, she was responsible for many goings-on there, but creating new dishes was her favorite pastime. Family, friends, and flavorful fragrances frequented the festive kitchen; it was where Chef delighted in demonstrating her culinary talents.

Determined to learn the importance of being a zester, Lester made the brave decision to explore his new home further. Once Chef's kitchen had closed for the evening, he slipped away in secret from the other sleeping tools in the Everyday Drawer.

The warm, sweet scents of citrus and freshly-baked bottom crust still mingled quietly above the dark galley. Moving cautiously along a moonlit marble countertop, Lester encountered an assembly of utensils socializing after hours.

"How do you do?" Lester offered Big Grater, the largest member of the group.

"I do very well. You're obviously new here, or you would already know that." Big Grater was 100% stainless steel and stood completely on his own. He boasted impressive, sharp holes on all four sides and could cut hefty foods like Russet potatoes and wedges of smelly cheese into long ribbons or strands.

Grater was grand and confident. During busy cooking weekends, he might not even return to the Everyday Drawer, remaining instead beside Chef's pastry board overnight. "Your cutting holes seem sadly small. Are you embarrassed by them? And what, precisely, are you staring at?"

Lester had not wished
to be impolite, but a
bit of food was drying
over one of Grater's
front holes, and he was
finding it most difficult
to look away. "You have
something orange,
stuck just there. I think
it's cheddar."

"He's right; it's cheddar!" shrieked Shredder. Looking less lustrous, Grater retreated to the rear of the group, where he fumbled frantically to free himself from the spoiled debris.

Shredder appeared much wider than Lester and had a fancy gripper handle made from all-natural wood. "I'm imported, you know. I was mass-produced at a factory in Taiwan, and I come with an extended warranty. Do you even know what that is?"

Lester blushed and
wondered if he,
too, had a warranty
extending somewhere
off of him.

"I don't believe so; it
sounds uncomfortable,"
he decided quietly.
Shredder shriveled.
Giggling at this
unexpected response
was the pretty and
petite Peeler.

Peeler was the quietest of the utensils gathered, but she wasn't at all dull. She could remove wide strips of skin from vegetables like carrots or cucumbers with a single blade, and she was particularly proud of her prominent place. "I've lived in the Everyday Drawer my entire life," she smiled.

Trying to stand
upright with the rest
of the tools was the
wobbling Pasta Wheel.
She had a fancy,
crimped spinning
wheel made of
genuine brass! Wheel
loved to roll lazily
through long sheets
of dough, perfecting
precise patterns
of pasta for Chef's
lasagna and ravioli.

Wheel believed that she might be gluten-free, though she wasn't exactly sure what that meant. Lester politely shared that he was also fond of pasta and was very happy to make her acquaintance.

An odd odor caused
Lester to turn in time to
see Garlic Press approach
from behind. Just GP to his
friends, Garlic Press was
a sleek, hand-held device
famous for pressing
pungent, pulpy paste from
cloves of garlic.

Made of a sturdy, die-cast construction, GP helped Chef prepare heart-healthy meals. "My ergonomic design makes me a joy to use. Plus, I'm dishwasher safe!" he recited from memory.

"Yes, we are all aware," barked Can Opener. "Now, if you could just do something about that smell!"

With his noisy mechanical parts, Lester thought Opener might be the most intimidating kitchen tool of all. When an electric current ran inside him, Opener could chew right through the tops of metal cans without a single pause. Curious to know more, Lester asked, "What can you do when you aren't plugged in?" The gang silently retreated from the naïve zester.

Opener evaluated Lester defensively for a moment, perhaps trying to determine who had sent this clever young device to humiliate him. "I was almost in a television commercial once," Opener rebounded. "You don't look electric to me. Where is your cord, man? Why, you're just another gadgety thing. You belong in the Gadget Box!"

A low, gasping sound echoed quickly around the dark kitchen. There it was—the unspeakable had been spoken. Opener had regretted saying it immediately, but there was no taking it back.

"It won't be long before he's sorted out to the Box forever," whispered the whirling whisk. From that moment, many of the kitchen characters kept a cookie-cutter's distance from Lester.

Back in the crowded
Everyday Drawer, but
feeling quite alone,
Lester tried to forget
his confrontation with
Opener. He imagined,
instead, his first important
zesting assignment.
Filled with expectation,
he scanned the kitchen in
his mind, trying to predict
what those special culinary
orders might be.

His thoughts rested on a beautiful ceramic bowl near the sink. It was filled with fresh oranges and lemons. Perhaps Chef would start Lester off with something simple, like grating an orange or two to make a sweet glaze for some breakfast scones. Maybe he'd be tasked with zesting a half-dozen lemons for a fine after-dinner tart or a cheesecake.

Didn't he also recall seeing a molded pan for making madeleines? Yes, that must be it; he could smell them baking already. Lester would be in charge of creating a dozen delightful madeleines! If only he could be certain how to do such things. Would Lester discover his true kitchen purpose in time, or spend a miserable life in the Gadget Box?

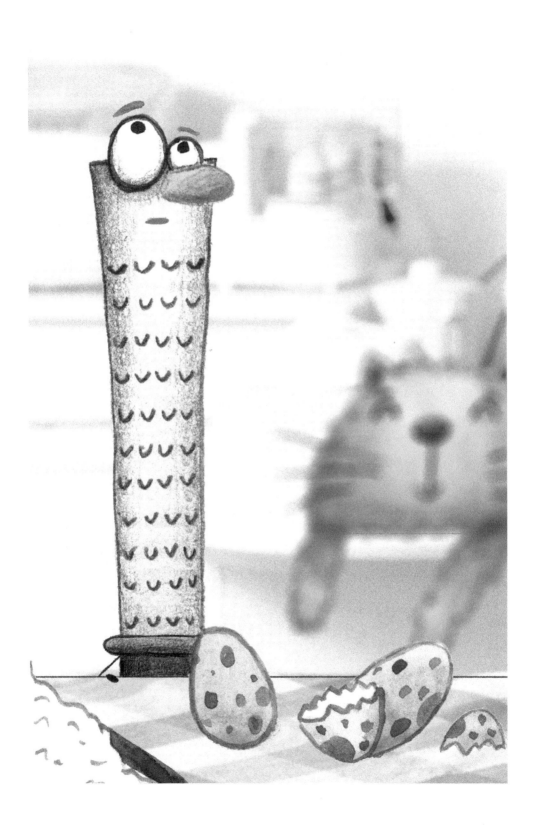

Lester stirred the next morning, feeling more anxious than ever. A kindly plastic spatula listened patiently as Lester recounted his misadventures from the night before. He offered some comforting words. "You may not understand your purpose just yet, but you're here now. That's a decent start. If I were you, I would have a talk with old Handy Mixer. He's lived in the kitchen longer than any of us, and he is very thoughtful. You'll find him one cupboard over."

"Thank you, sir. How long did it take for you to find your kitchen purpose?"

"That was easy," Spatula smiled through his slender slots. "I'm a spatula! You know: Slide-lift-flip, slide-lift-flip, all day long. Now, off you go."

Not wanting to lose another moment, Lester tiptoed toward a napping tenderizer and past a pair of chatting chopsticks until he was free from his place in the Drawer. He knocked gently on the neighboring container before entering.

Handy Mixer came to live in the kitchen many holidays before this one, a gift from Chef's grandmother. Having lost his fine metallic finish some time ago (from being so useful and so loved for so long), Mixer now resided in a small cupboard dedicated to classic, care-worn things. Of all the kitchen tools, he was respected as clever and wise. He greeted Lester with a mature countenance and a thoughtful smile.

Hoping for many answers to many things, Lester momentarily forgot his manners. "Mixer, am I modern? Lately, I wonder if I shouldn't wish for a plug-in cord, like Toaster, or a spinning blade, like Blender." He then noticed that Mixer had none of these things, either.

Mixer regarded Lester's impatience with kindness. "What is the question you truly wish to ask?"

Lester closed his eyes and tried to steady himself. From somewhere inside, he heard his voice escape as a fragile whisper: "Am I *wanted*?"

Mixer smiled. "You are special as you are, Lester. A zester has much to offer; you have been given smaller holes for a reason. With them, you can create lovely, fine, and delicate things, like velvety shavings that release subtle aromas and flavors. Your unique teeth will help Chef to craft feathery, flakey textures from cinnamon, nutmeg, citrus, and chocolate. She would not trust these important tasks with any other tool. This is your kitchen purpose, Lester. You do not need moveable parts or a shiny handle to matter. You are beautiful and loved for your simplicity."

Lester pondered Handy Mixer's words for a moment. "I do love chocolate," he mused. "But...will there be enough room for me to live forever in the Everyday Drawer?" he worried.

"We are all different, but there is room in the kitchen for each of us. Chef has already made a place for you." Upon hearing this, Lester was greatly relieved.

Lester thought a bit further. "But what becomes of those who are sent away to live in the Gadget Box? Does such a horrible place really exist?"

"Each of us must determine the true nature of our usefulness, our reason for being. What will our unique gifts to the kitchen be? Chef does not sort one tool from another, Lester. Ultimately, we sort ourselves, according to whether or not we *believe*. A Gadget Box, or even an Everyday Drawer, isn't really a place, after all. These are simply a frame of mind. As we believe what we can (or cannot) be, we also choose our place in the world. This is a lot for a young tool to consider. Do you understand, Lester?"

"I think so. But what keeps some tools from believing?"

"Envy and regret, mostly. These are like unwanted ingredients. If you are not careful, they will reveal themselves and spoil anything you hope to create." Lester couldn't recall seeing these things in the kitchen, but he made a note to himself to steer clear of them in the future.

"You are a zester with great potential, Lester. It's now up to you to become the very best that you can be."

That night, Lester
slept well for the first
time since arriving
at Chef's home.
Early the very next
morning, his presence
was requested in the
kitchen, no doubt for
something *grate*! For
many holiday seasons
to come, Lester would
feel loved and useful.

Once he had learned to believe in himself, the rest of the kitchen believed in him, too. Lester was happy to have found the true meaning of being a zester, and, as Mixer had promised, there was room in the kitchen for every tool. None were exactly alike, yet each belonged. Lester lived his life with purpose and made the very most of his *grate* adventures!

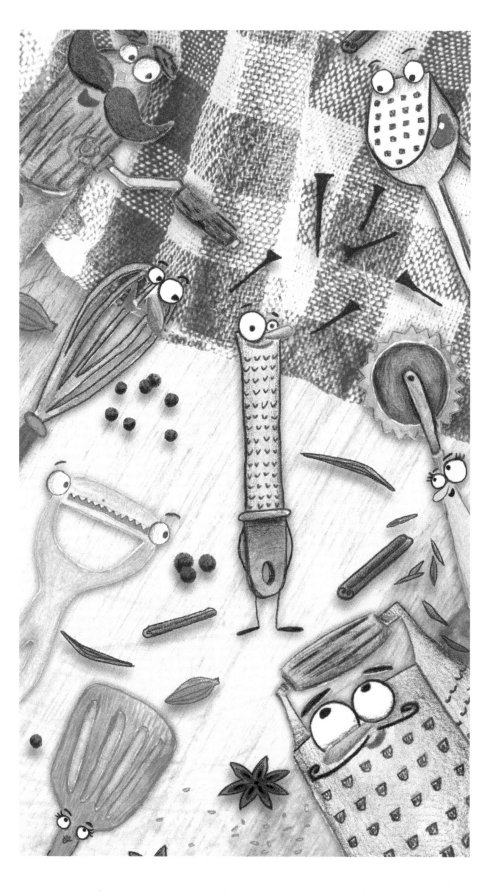

Lester Zester has a new adventure ahead. Have you uncovered an urgent message?

Lightning Source UK Ltd.
Milton Keynes UK
UKHW050435061021
391712UK00003B/144

9 781645 383000